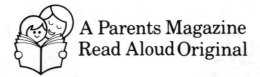

Leon's Prize

by Jerry Smath

Parents Magazine Press ♥ New York

To my grandson, Ian James Miller,
with love—J.S.

Library of Congress Cataloging-in-Publication Data

Smath, Jerry.
Leon's prize / by Jerry Smath.
        p.   cm.
Summary: Leon learns that having all the
dance prizes in the world means nothing
next to having the one he loves.

ISBN 0-8193-1169-3
[1. Dancing—Fiction.]   I. Title
PZ7.S6393Le 1987
[E]—dc19   87-25800
                                            CIP
                                            AC

"Today is the day," said Emily.

"Where are you going?" asked Leon.
"It's a secret!" said Emily.
She kissed Leon goodbye and
rushed out the door.

Later, Emily returned with a big package.
"Surprise, dear Leon!" she said.
"Did you forget that
today is your birthday?"
Leon quickly opened the package.

"A phonograph! How wonderful!"
he exclaimed.
Leon put a record on the phonograph.
"May I have this dance?" he asked.

Emily and Leon danced well together.
They wiggled and jiggled
and bounced all around.
They were very good indeed.

Leon was so excited that
he ran to get the newspaper.

"Look, there are four dance contests
being held today," he said.
"Let's go! We could have lots of fun."

Emily agreed.
So, off they both went
to the first dance.

At the Bunny Hug Ball,
they wiggled and jiggled
and hopped up and down.

They were very good and won a gold cup.
All the bunnies clapped their paws
with delight.

The cup was too heavy for Leon to carry,
so Emily borrowed a wagon from
one of the bunnies.
"You are very good to me," Leon said.
"Now let's go to the Whooping Crane Hop."

At the hop, they wiggled and jiggled
and danced high above the ground.

They were very good, and won
a second gold cup.
All the cranes flapped their wings
and whooped with delight.

"I like dancing more than anything else!
Don't you, Emily?" asked Leon.
Emily only smiled.

"Now, let's go on to the Crawfish Crawl,"
said Leon.

When they got there, the place was empty,
except for a turtle sitting on a rock.
When Leon asked where the dance was,
the turtle pointed down into the river.
"It's underwater!" said Emily.
"We will surely drown!"
"No problem," said Leon.
"We will breathe through these straws."

Leon jumped into the river,
pulling Emily in after him.

At the Crawfish Crawl,
they wiggled and jiggled
and bubbled around.
They were very good and won
a third gold cup.
All the crawfish clicked their clampers
with delight.

"I could dance with you all day,"
said Leon. "Isn't this fun?"
"Yes, it is," replied Emily.
"But I think it's time we went home."
"There's only one dance left," said Leon.
"Come on! Let's go to the
Billy Goat Bash."

"Oh, my!" sighed Emily.
"I'll never be able to climb that high."
"No problem," said Leon. "Just
take my paw."

Leaving the wagon below,
he helped pull Emily up
the steep mountain.

At the top, the Billy Goat Bash
was in full swing.

They wiggled and jiggled
and jumped around.
Again they were very good, and won
a fourth gold cup.
All the billy goats butted their horns
with delight.

"This is the most fun I've ever had!
How about you, Emily?" asked Leon.
Emily didn't answer. She looked worried.
"How will we get back down?" she asked.

"No problem," said Leon.
"Just take my paw and I will help you."
But as they started to go...

...Emily slipped and started to fall.
"Help!" she screamed.

Down she fell,

bouncing and bumping,

bumping and bouncing all the way.

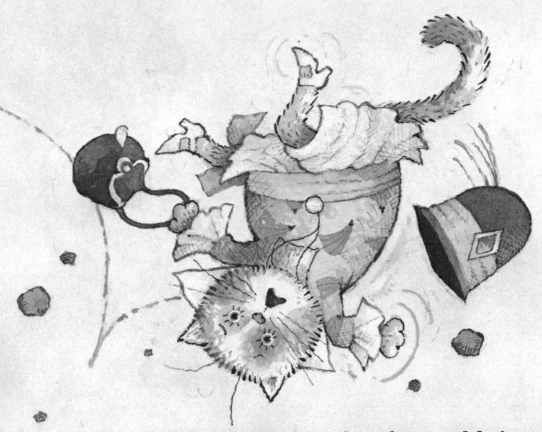

Leon tried to stop her, but he couldn't.

"Emily! Emily! Are you all right?"
cried Leon.
"Speak to me!"
"I'll be fine," said Emily, "as soon as
I catch my breath."

Leon suddenly began throwing all the
gold cups out of the wagon.
"What are you doing?" asked Emily.
"Aren't you going to take the prizes home?"
"NO!" said Leon...

"...for *you* are my prize, dear Emily,
and the only one I wish to take home."
Leon started to pull the wagon
and Emily smiled.
"You are very good to me," she said.

About the Author

Jerry Smath once had five cats—a mother
and her four kittens. But although the
cats did lots of silly things around the
house, Mr. Smath *never* caught them dancing.

Mr. Smath has written and illustrated
many books for children, among them *But
No Elephants, Up Goes Mr. Down,* and *The
Housekeeper's Dog* for Parents. He and
his wife, Valerie, live in Westchester
County, New York.